If Daddy
Only Knew Me

LILA McGINNIS
Illustrations by DIANE PATERSON

ALBERT WHITMAN & COMPANY • Morton Grove, Illinois

Library of Congress Cataloging-in-Publication Data

McGinnis, Lila.
    If Daddy only knew me / written by Lila McGinnis;
illustrated by Diane Paterson.
        p.   cm.
    Summary: Curious about the father who left them
years ago, five-year-old Kate and her older sister,
Glory, make an expedition across town to view him
at his new home where he has a new family.
    ISBN 0-8075-3537-0
    (1. Divorce—Fiction. 2. Fathers and daughters—
Fiction.) I. Paterson, Diane, 1946–   ill. II. Title.
PZ7.M478475If   1995
(E)—dc20   95-3135
                                                          CIP
                                                          AC

Published in 1995 by Albert Whitman & Company,
6340 Oakton Street, Morton Grove, Illinois 60053.
Published simultaneously in Canada by
General Publishing, Limited, Toronto.
Printed in Canada.
10 9 8 7 6 5 4 3 2 1

The text typeface is Benguiat.
The illustrations are rendered in watercolor.
Design by Susan B. Cohn.

For my children, who never doubted.
L.M.

For Betsy and Jana, who sailed through
the storm and learned how to fly.
D.P.

Now I'm five. I go to kindergarten. That's where I figured out that everyone knows about their daddy.

Everyone but us.

"I know," my sister, Glory, said when I told her.

"Liar! You don't even know where he lives! Tom's daddy lives in Cleveland. Mary's daddy lives at her house."

"Our daddy lives on Seventh Street," my sister said. "Didn't you know that, silly Kate?"

"No," I said. "You don't know it, either. Justin's daddy works at the post office and wears a blue shirt with a patch."

"Our daddy wears a blue suit." Glory banged two keys on the piano. "Sometimes jeans," she said, and banged two more.

I asked my mother then, because Glory makes things up sometimes.

"It's true, Kate," Mom said. "Glory is right. And he does live on Seventh Street."

Then she hugged me so hard I couldn't breathe.

"You know he moved away when you were just this big." She made a little circle with her hands.

"But why?"

"Because." She pushed the hair out of my eyes and smiled at me. "He changed his mind. He didn't want a family anymore. I should have told you sooner, but I didn't want to talk about it. I didn't want you to be sad." She kissed the tip of my nose.

"At least he sends the checks on time," she said, and kissed the top of my head.

"Last year he changed his mind again, and now he has a new family. But I love you, Kate," she said. "Grandpa loves you, and Grandma and Glory love you. Your friends love you. You don't need a daddy."

But I did.

If I had a daddy of my own, I could tell about him at school.

We could hike in the woods by the river.

We could laugh, a lot.

If I had a daddy, maybe he would hate green beans, too, and we wouldn't have to eat them.

"Don't waste your tears," Glory said that night when we went to bed. "He can stay on Seventh Street."

"I'm not crying. Don't be dumb." I wiped my sleeve across my eyes, in case. "Where is Seventh Street?" I asked.

"I don't remember. It's clear across town, too far to walk."

"It's important," I said. "Can't we go and look at him?"

"Shut up and go to sleep," she answered, and rolled over so I couldn't see her face.

On Saturday she whispered, "Let's go, while Mom is cleaning house."

It *was* too far to walk. We went all the way to Main Street and turned.

First Street.

Second Street—my toes tingled in my shoes. My eyes blinked at the white, sunshiny sidewalk.

"Want to go home?" Glory asked.

"No," I said. "Will he know who we are?"

"How could he? When he lived with us, all you did was crawl around and wet your diapers."

She pulled me under a striped awning in front of a doughnut store to rest a minute.

"My hair was light then, like yours," she said. "Now it's short and dark like his, but he doesn't know that. Don't worry, he won't know us."

At Fourth Street we waited for an ice-cream truck to turn the corner.

"Is he nice?" I asked. She raised her eyebrows and didn't answer.

Fifth Street.

Sixth Street.

We crossed on the green light. We were almost there.

Seventh Street.

When we turned the corner, I held my breath and forgot to let it out. Glory punched my arm.

"Breathe," she said.

I did.

"Mom showed me his house one day. It's dark green," she said. "But he won't even be home, I bet."

He was mowing the grass.

"Are you sure that's him?"

"Of course I'm sure."

He pushed the mower, back and forth, back and forth across the yard. We stood by the fire-plug and watched.

He wore a blue sweater and jeans, just like anybody.

His hair was dark like Glory's. It curled like hers.

He didn't look at us.

Glory forgot to breathe this time. I poked her.

"Happy now?" she asked. "Can we go home?"

"Not yet." I wanted to stay a bit, in case.

Then Glory grabbed my arm. "Look," she said and pointed.

A stroller with a white roof sat by the front steps.

"Since we're here we might as well see his new baby." She pulled me right up the sidewalk past the mower.

We peeked in the stroller and there it was, wide awake.

"Don't touch him, kids," our daddy said. He stopped the mower and came over beside us.

"Nice baby," Glory said in a funny voice. She rubbed her hand across her cheek.

I squinted up at Daddy's face. When he smiled at the baby, I saw one tooth was chipped.

His eyes were blue like ours.

Bits of grass hung on his jeans. I didn't brush them off. I made a fist in my pocket, instead.

"Is that the only kid you have?" asked Glory.

My dad grinned. "Just the one," he said.

He cooed funny sounds at the baby, and I looked at Glory. Her blue eyes were squeezed shut. One tear got out, anyhow.

I grabbed her hand. "Come on, Glory," I said.
"We have to get home."
"About time," she answered, backing off.

"Glory?" said our dad. He said something else, but we were half-across the yard by then; we kept walking.

He stared after us. I know. I looked back.

We didn't run. We just walked down the sidewalk.

When Glory turned her head, he was still watching us.

On Main Street, we ran:

Sixth Street,

Fifth Street,

Fourth Street, and clear to the store at the corner, where we knew our way home with our eyes closed, practically.

At our house Mom stood in the driveway. As we got close she folded her arms and glared at us.

"Well?" she said. "Where have you been?"

We told her, and she closed her eyes and shook her head.

"Don't you ever go that far away again all by yourselves," she said at last, and put her arms around us and hugged us.

Then she gave us lemonade and cookies.

"Why doesn't Daddy love us?" I asked.

"Because he doesn't know you," she said slowly. "And he never wants to know you because he's afraid if he did, he would love you."

"That's dumb," I said. "He's not afraid to love that new baby. Why can't he love his old babies?"

"He did, once," my mother said.

"Long time ago," said Glory, and she gave me Bear to hold.

"Maybe he thinks his heart won't stretch far enough to let everyone in," she said. Then she stretched her arms wide and hugged Bear and me until we giggled.

"He doesn't know what he's missing," said Mom. She poured more lemonade and pushed the plate of cookies across the table. "He doesn't know you are the best reader in your class, Glory."

"Yes, and he doesn't know Kate can skip," she answered.

"He doesn't know I can say my letters backwards," I said, and then I chose the cookie with the most chocolate chips.

"My heart stretches," I told them. "Mine has room for loving everybody."

"Except him, I bet," said Glory.

I squeezed Bear tight; he didn't mind.

"I'll have to think about that," I said, but I knew already. Even if he liked green beans, I would stretch a place for him. In case.